For
Sebastian
with love

Copyright © 1992 by Helen Craig

First U.S. edition 1992
First published in Great Britain in 1992
by Walker Books Ltd., London.
ISBN 1-56402-102-5

Library of Congress Cataloging-in-Publication Data:
Craig Helen,
The town mouse and the country mouse / by Helen Craig. —1st U.S. ed.
Summary: When a town mouse and a country mouse
exchange visits, they find that they prefer very different ways of life.
ISBN 1-56402-102-5 (hardcover)
[1. Fables. 2. Mice—Fiction.] I. Title.
PZ8.2.C69To 1992   91-58761
[E]—dc20

10 9 8 7 6 5 4 3 2 1

Printed and bound in Belguim

The artwork for this book consists of ink and
watercolor paintings.

Candlewick Press
2067 Massachusetts Avenue
Cambridge, Massachusetts 02140

THE TOWN MOUSE AND THE COUNTRY MOUSE

Retold and illustrated by HELEN CRAIG

CANDLEWICK PRESS
CAMBRIDGE, MASSACHUSETTS

Once upon a time deep in the hedgerow there lived a country mouse called Charlie. One afternoon he was sitting at his window listening to a blackbird singing while the sun warmed the fur on his back, when there was a knock at the door. It was his cousin, Tyler the town mouse.

"Hi there, Charlie! I've come to visit," said Tyler, marching in and flopping down in Charlie's best armchair. "I'm exhausted. What a trip! Anything to eat?"

Charlie got him a bowl of nuts and marigold seeds topped with some red hawthorn berries that he had been saving for a special treat. But Tyler wrinkled his nose. "Boring," he said. "Still, I suppose it's good for you."

When he had finished eating, he leaned back. "Now, Charlie, is there anything going on around here in the evenings?" Charlie smiled. "Yes, there is. I'll take you to see something wonderful."

That evening they
climbed the hill behind
Charlie's house.
The sun was just going
down, and all the birds
were singing their best
songs. They waited
while the sky filled with
brilliant colors.
"There!" whispered Charlie.
"Where?" said Tyler.

"The sunset," said Charlie.
"Isn't it beautiful?"
Tyler yawned. "Too slow
for me. I like a little action."
And he took off down the hill.

That night Tyler couldn't sleep. The countryside was just too dark and quiet.

The next morning when he saw that breakfast was nuts, seeds, and berries again, he decided enough was enough.

"Sorry, Charlie," he said. "Country life is not for me. I need the bright lights of the town. But why not come back with me and see how exciting life can be?"

Charlie had never been farther
than the top of the hill,
but he said bravely, "All right,
I will. Just let me pack a few
things and lock up the house."
And they set off.

They had not gone far
when they met a
carrier pigeon.
"I'm on my way to town,"
she said. "Would you
like a lift? Climb aboard
and hold on tight!"

As they soared high into the air, Charlie watched his hedgerow get smaller and smaller until it disappeared. He felt very lost.

It was a long journey.
At last the carrier pigeon
set them down in the town
marketplace. Charlie stood
rooted to the spot. There
were so many people;
there was so much noise.

"Come on, Charlie," hissed Tyler, dragging
him into the safety of the shadows.

"It's dangerous here.
Stick close
and follow me."

They scuttled off, along a gutter,

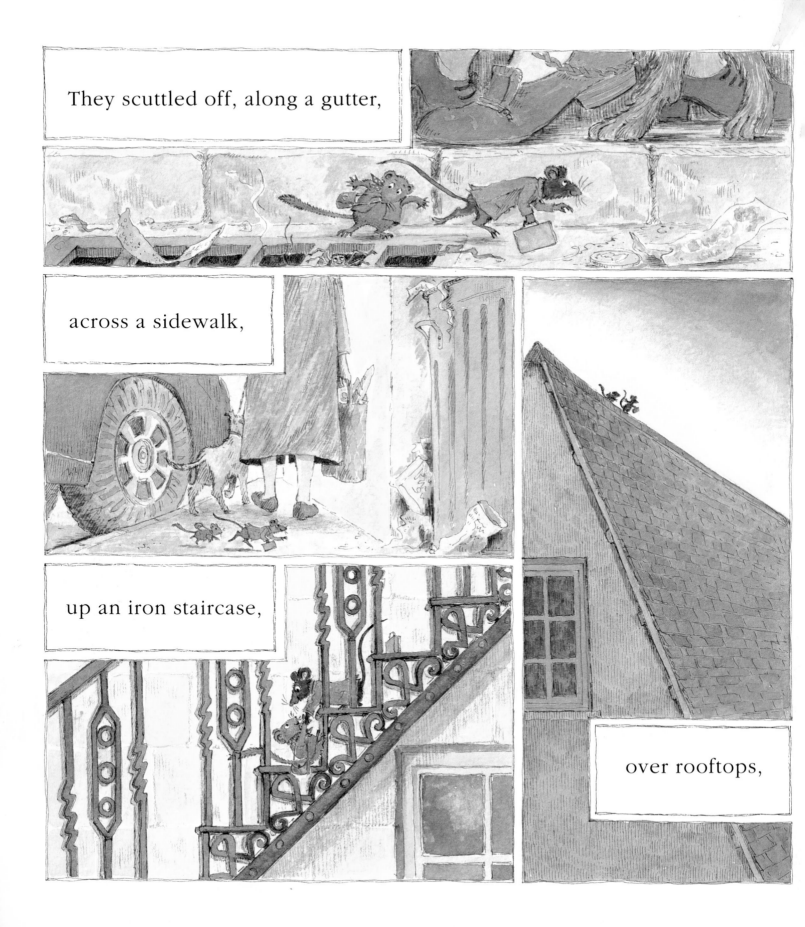

across a sidewalk,

up an iron staircase,

over rooftops,

down a chimney,

and through a window.

At the end of a musty passage, bright light streamed from a small hole.

"In we go," whispered Tyler, and he squeezed through. Charlie followed.

Aaaah! A giant cat with fierce eyes and huge sharp teeth was waiting to pounce on them! **"Help!"** squealed Charlie.

He swayed and fell, but Tyler caught him by the tail. He was laughing. "Don't be silly, Charlie. We're in a theater. It's only a movie."

Poor Charlie peeped through his paws. The giant cat was now chasing a giant mouse. It was all very strange.

The movie ended and
they set off again
through the dark streets.
On the way Charlie
nearly got squashed …

gassed …

drowned in a
sea of paper …

and knocked out by
a runaway pineapple.

"You must be more careful!" said Tyler, picking him up for the fourth time.

Charlie was very glad when they reached the steps of the big house where Tyler lived.

"I bet you're hungry," said Tyler, leading the way to the dining room. "Let's see what's left." And he dashed around the table looking for the best food. "Have some sardines and chocolate mousse," he said.

"How about shrimp in mayonnaise or prunes and pudding?"

He offered Charlie sausages, ice cream, and a piece of fatty bacon.

"Have a drink!" he called, knocking over a wine glass. Charlie didn't like any of it much. He was beginning to feel very sick and dizzy.

Suddenly there was a horrible noise.
Yeowwoull!
Thump!
A fat cat landed on the table.
Tyler vanished.

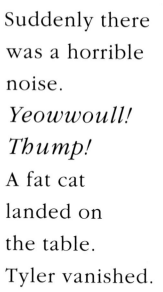

The cat sprang.
Charlie jumped.

The cat chased him around and around and up and down,

until Charlie dived under a sofa and scuttled up into one of the springs.

The cat could smell Charlie.
Charlie could smell the cat.
The cat watched the sofa for a
long, long time. Charlie waited,
trembling. He thought his
end had come and he would
never see his comfortable
home in the hedgerow again.

At last he heard the cat being shooed out and almost at once Tyler appeared.

"Sorry, Charlie. Forgot to tell you where the mouse hole was. Are you all right? You look a little odd."

And he led Charlie through a hole under the sideboard and put him to bed.

Charlie had nightmares all night.

Very early in the morning Charlie woke Tyler and said, "I'm sorry. Town life is just too much for me. I think I'd better go home."

So Tyler took him back to the market-place and put him on a milk van that was going to the farm near the hedgerow.

Charlie was so pleased to be home again. He ate a large dish of red hawthorn berries while the blackbird sang and the sun warmed the fur on his back.

That night Tyler put on his top hat, white tie, and tails and went across town for some fun at the theater. He was very happy.

Under the same night sky, Charlie lay on his hill. He had watched the sun set, and now he was counting the stars. He was very happy too!